PENINSULA

S.M. FLANAGAN

This edition first published in paperback by
Michael Terence Publishing in 2023
www.mtp.agency

Copyright © 2023 S.M. Flanagan

S.M. Flanagan has asserted the right to be identified as
the author of this work in accordance with the
Copyright, Designs and Patents Act 1988

ISBN 9781800945296

No part of this publication may be reproduced, stored
in a retrieval system, or transmitted, in any form or
by any means, electronic, mechanical, photocopying,
recording or otherwise, without the prior
permission of the publisher

Cover image
Copyright © Quangpraha
www.123rf.com

Cover design
Copyright © 2023 Michael Terence Publishing

Contents

Introduction 1
Introduction (Introductory) 3
Introduction (Introductory) A Disturbed Monique's Defiance 4
Foreword 6
1: Nazi Ideals 7
2: Monique's Defiance 10
3: Another War Film and Another Joke 13
4: Spanish Dreams (A Vision) 15
5: The Followers of Nazism 19
6: The Beer Cellar 22
7: Monique's Ambivalence 24
8: Family Love 27
9: Cry Baby 30
10: Both Sisters Run Over to Church 32
11: Family Holiday (A Blissful Paradise) 35
12: A Miracle (Dream) 47
13: Monique's Introspective 49
14: Monique's Nazi Recrimination 51
15: Monique's Punctual Departure 55
16: Cosmopolitan Citizen (Spanish Days and Life) ... 57
17: Monique's Beach Life and Times at Peninsula ... 60
18: A Peninsula Dream 63
Also by S.M. Flanagan 65

Introduction

In her bedroom, Monique stood by the wardrobe's mirrored door with her Blonde Mother. A concerned parent. Monique looked at herself in the mirror. She saw her narcissistic mirrored reflection.

"Why am I German? Why can't I be another Nationality? I am ashamed of my race. My Nationality," grumbled Daughter.

"You are what you are. You should be proud of your Nationality. You should be proud," stated Mother.

With anger, Monique objected to it.

"What? A damn Nazi! What's there to be proud of."

"Look! You must love yourself. Take pride in yourself. I admit it's not the best history. You must be proud. Don't let history get you down."

"I will emigrate. That's what!" grumbled Monique. "Be a foreigner in a new country."

"I wish you luck!" said Mother patronisingly.

Monique's Mother came out of her daughter's bedroom. Going downstairs.

Monique opened the wardrobe door. She squeezed into the wardrobe. She sat down in the corner of the dark wardrobe. Monique spent her time reflecting on her nationality. She would take the necessary measures to emigrate if permitted and allowed.

Monique was outraged by her country. (Nation's History.)

Monique felt ashamed of herself and her nationality. In the silence, Monique stayed in a corner of the wardrobe huddled up.

She had a childish girl's tantrum. She sulked. Monique was disturbed and distressed. Monique cooled off by staying inside her wardrobe. At that time the light turned dark. Her bedroom became dark.

Introduction (Introductory)

In her bedroom standing still by a dressing table mirror, Monique looked at herself vainly. She disliked herself. She disapproved of her nationality of actually being German. She detested it. Typically, she had typical xenophobia. She had a xenophobic detestation!

Of course, Monique would do anything to be another race or nationality. Therefore, to live in another country abroad would definitely solace her and make her relieved. Of course, it was pleasing to her without a doubt. Did it remain a fantasy? A dream? Was it a reality? An aspiratory unfulfillment. Only time would tell if it was a realistic dream!

Monique prayed and hoped her dream would come true. Her dream ended up being a miracle. Monique dreamt. Her dream came true! She aspired.

It was a miraculous transformation to one's own life. According to Monique's experiences, it remained a remarkable testimony! A heartfelt testament which she gave testimony at church one Sunday evening. At a Sunday service.

Introduction (Introductory)
A Disturbed Monique's Defiance

Monique came out of her bedroom. She came downstairs. She burst into the Lounge. There she found members of her family gathered together. Unashamed, Monique spoke. She confronted them. Monique was disturbed. At first, her voice was soft. She raised her tone of voice so she could be clearly heard. With defiance she addressed an issue,

"I don't want any part of it. I don't want to be oppressed. To live in oppression. Things are too oppressive as it stands right now. My life. How I live my life. Everything about life and society. I will rebel and revolt against it. I shall live my life and be free. I shall leave this country and be freed from it." Said Monique defiantly.

"I do understand how you feel. It's understandable. You don't like your life. You are ashamed. Oh! Dear! We would like to help you with this. We are serious. We will get to the bottom of this," said Mother sympathetically.

Monique's family thought of the insubordinate and insurgent public, citizens, civilian inhabitants, and countrymen. An insurgency and insubordination amongst the general public. How times had drastically changed with revolt, rebellion, insurgency, insurrection and insubordination nowadays in today's society.

"I will leave this country if it's the very last thing I do. I assure you I will leave. I promise you," concluded Monique unashamedly.

"We wish you well," they said.

Monique spoke in a sarcastic tone of voice.

"Do you. How nice!" said Monique sarcastically.

Foreword

It was an ancestral tendency of theirs. Their Ancestors kept old diaries. Throughout the generations. Families read their Ancestors' entries. They of course learned about their Ancestors' lives and experiences. Including Monique, a Grand-daughter too.

Despite having xenophobia, Monique became a xenophobe of being German and of course from its History. (She used to know acquaintances from DRESDEN.)

Now due to circumstances beyond her control, it was time for Monique to relinquish her GERMAN citizenship. Her Nationality. Her xenophobia for it still did remain. Her ideal dream was to live in PENINSULA . . .

1
Nazi Ideals

Monique opened her compact and looked at the small mirror. Monique looked at her face. The beautiful makeup. Hours earlier Monique had applied her makeup.

Monique looked at herself in gratified narcissism. With self-love for herself, she took narcissistic joy in gratifying from her vainness!

At midday, Monique came out alone into the garden that summer. At that time the sun shone hotter. With a thrill, Monique felt excited from her narcissism. Monique took the opportunity to sunbathe out in the garden alone. She lay down on a blanket on the lawn. There she sunbathed. She tanned in the heat. Her suntan was bronze. Her beautiful sandy, fair hair was golden.

Monique was dehydrated and sweltered in the sweltering sun. She felt enervated at being exposed to the hot sun. She perspired. From perspiration, Monique sweltered when sunbathing.

At this time of day, she preferred the actual peace and quiet of the daytime. Also, her privacy and seclusion too.

The German Blonde enjoyed her erotomania. Monique took pleasure in her eroticism. She took narcissism from her virginal beauty. A virgin beauty's narcissism!

Monique engaged in narcissistic thoughts. Monique closed her eyes. She lounged in the sun. As a result of applying suntan lotion onto her beautiful body. Her lovely suntan got darker and her hair glossy. She was beautified in the radiant sun. Monique was beautifying from suntanning and sunbathing herself. The narcissist beatified. Of vain contemplation and self-love of oneself! The narcissistic sunbather took joy!

After about a few hours later Monique got up from the lawn. She stood up. She felt dehydrated and enervated. She felt thirsty. Her throbbing veins and her temple pulsated. She was dazed while standing still. She put on her sandals. From somewhere in the garden there she walked back to the house.

Entering the Lounge there Monique found her Father alone sitting in the armchair while reading a newspaper. Monique stood in front of her distracted Father. The Daughter questioned her Father. Monique pressed for an answer.

"Well. Am I an Arian?" asked Daughter.

"Haven't we been through this before? What makes you say that?"

"Well. Am I?" prompted Daughter.

With concern, Monique's Father answered the question.

"Your Ancestors are from Hitler's Youth," answered Father.

"Well. Are they? Should I be proud of it? My nationality," said Daughter ashamedly.

Monique's Father was unanswered.

Was her Father unashamed and too proud?

Monique walked to the dining table. There she got her handbag which was left on top of the table. She took out a notepad.

"I have made some notes. Arian is a super race. It's Hitler's ideology. It is the Master Race. The Third Reich built on the Fuhrer's ultimate dream!"

Standing still Monique wondered about it. Did she have mixed emotions? Was Monique appalled and disgusted? Or was she unashamed and proud like her Father? The Fatherland!

With a sense of outrage or pride, she must have felt. The Daughter left her Father at once. Going upstairs to her bedroom. Monique lay down on her luxury bed and rested in her shady, cool bedroom. The bed sheets were soiled and stained from the suntan lotion on her body rubbing against them.

2
Monique's Defiance

In the lounge, Monique and her younger sister Imogen sat together on a settee. Monique spent time looking at a photo album. Now she had already seen this photo album many times. Monique admired the lovely photographs. Their Blonde parents were beautifully photographed.

"It's really hard to believe. My Ancestors are from Hitler's Youth!" reflected Monique.

"It really is expected, isn't it? It's History. That's our Ancestors," said Sister matter-of-factly.

Monique expressed her defiance for being a German citizen of German Nationality.

"Is this what we are part of? It's our ancestral background. I am not proud. I am sick! There's nothing to be proud of being a NAZI in NAZI GERMANY. And then there's the Hitler's Youth movement," said Monique defiantly.

"They are proud. They are proud of being German. Me. My eyes are dark. I am no blue-eyed blonde!" said Imogen unashamedly.

Monique was a natural golden blonde. Naturally, her long hair was flaxen in the natural sunlight. Monique was conceited and narcissistic. After all, she had a beautiful natural blondeness.

"Isn't it crazy this ideology and doctrine? I love myself. I am proud of myself. I dislike my nationality. I will emigrate. Be something else. I jolly well have to be. Another Nationality probably," said Monique admittedly.

Imogen mentioned her failing.

"Neither am I proud of being German. It's a stigma," admitted Sister.

Without a doubt, Monique remained uncertain about something.

"Are Germans proud?" asked Monique.

"I don't know. I guess some are," replied Imogen.

With deep regret, Monique expressed her discontentment.

"Me. I am not. I know some people who are proud Germans. They are proud of their country. Their Fatherland."

Imogen a bigot got up and left her sister alone. Within minutes Monique sitting at a corner of the settee resting her head against it had nodded off. About hours later Monique felt much better after she had rested. Monique recovered. She came into the study. She took out an Encyclopaedia antique reference book from the bottom of the cabinet shelf.

Monique sat down on a swivel chair at the desk. She read up on Hitler's Youth. NAZI HISTORY. She gained knowledge by reading about the Arian. THE MASTER RACE. This ideology and doctrine combined both NAZISM and Arianism.

Staying upstairs. Relaxing in her bedroom alone. Monique reflected on it. Monique could not overcome her outrage. She may have been appalled or a proud citizen!

She felt disgusted at her Nationality. Wanting to be another Nationality. Wishing to be Spanish!

That's a wishful desire of hers!

Therefore, to emigrate abroad to Spain.

3
Another War Film and Another Joke

Monique came into the Lounge. At that time there she saw her Father watching television. A war film. He took pleasurable enjoyment in watching it.

Monique came to the conclusion that war films were stigmas and taboos. Monique became embarrassed at being German. Her German nationality remained an embarrassment. (Predominantly for the Germans and Germanic.)

She thought Second World War films were historically educational and caused corruption. Monique felt outraged and stigmatised by war films and their customaries.

"It's the bloody same thing over and over again. The goodies win the war and the baddies lose," grumbled Daughter.

The distracted Father got displeasure as his Daughter spoiling his enjoyment of watching the film.

"Don't talk to me. I am trying to watch the film. Can you get out of my way," moaned Father.

Monique remained unenthusiastic at joining her Father to watch the film together. He remained apathetic about watching the film together with his daughter.

Monique was a peacemaker. She disliked war films. She had a passion for romance. Monique was a romanticist and a dreamer.

Feeling unwanted Monique left the Lounge. She came into the clean kitchen. She got her sweets. Going upstairs. She went to her Brother's bedroom. In there, Tomas was engrossed in reading a comic. Tomas was distracted by his sister who came into his bedroom. Monique kindly offered her Brother some sweets. Tomas took a handful of sweets from a pack of sweets.

"What did Joker say to Batman?" joked Brother.

"Well, what did Joker say?"

Tomas told a joke.

Facing her Brother while she stood still. Monique put her hands on her hips gracefully. Finding it funny Monique burst out laughing at her Brother telling her a corny joke. Her laughter was childish and girlish. Monique was amused at her Brother's sense of humour. Leaving her Brother's bedroom. Monique laughed. In hysterics when she went to her bedroom.

4
Spanish Dreams (A Vision)

Monique came to see her Aunt at her home. In the dining room, they had tea together in comfort. Monique liked the treat which her Aunt provided. A nice tea. After eating her tea Monique rose and left the dining table. She sat down in the armchair while her restful Aunt sat down on the settee.

Monique took delight in comfort. She luxuriated in a comfortable seated position. Her tired Aunt relaxed after a long day today.

Monique took an interest in something. Monique picked up a photo album from a table. With interest, she looked at it. The family photo album. It consisted of family photographs. Monique had already seen this photo album many times. Losing interest in it, she put it back down on the table with a pile of magazines.

Monique wondered with interest.

"Can you tell me anything about my Ancestors? I would really like to know," said Monique inquisitively.

"What is there you would like to know?"

"I would really like to know anything about my Ancestors," replied Monique.

Monique's Aunt spoke about the Family Tree. Her Aunt focused on their Ancestors.

"Ladd and Linz were Nazis. They were once from Hitler's Youth. They both joined Hitler's rally. They belonged to Hitler's Youth. They both were good Nazis in Nazi Germany. They were loyal and patriotic to the state. Both Blonde!"

"Were they really? Shocking I say. I am not sure if I like this. Should I be proud?" said Monique indignantly.

"This was Nazism back then."

Monique seemed horrified and disgusted. She was outraged at the outrageous Nazis. Learning from Nazi History, she abhorred it. She certainly would do anything whatsoever therefore to be another Nationality. She was ashamed of being German!

Monique bent down and picked up her handbag. She opened her handbag and took out her compact. She opened it and looked at her face in the mirror. Did she love herself? She was a beautiful young German woman. Or did she hate herself?

"I don't like what I see," tutted Monique.

Stretching out, the Aunt touched Monique's fair hair. It was a golden brilliance in the radiant shining sunlight.

"You are so lovely," complimented Aunt.

"Oh! Am I really? I don't think I am. A NAZI. A German. This life is not for me," doubted Monique.

The Aunt encouraged a sense of pride.

"You must be proud of yourself. You must be proud of being German!" said Aunt proudly.

Monique closed her compact firmly. She frowned.

"No. I am not," scowled Monique.

"You shouldn't blame yourself. Do love yourself. Be proud. Don't let history get in the way."

"Me! Never! It makes me sick! I don't wish to be part of it. They are Nazis! I am not," glowered Monique.

The Aunt was reasonable in her reasoning.

"You can't change history. Can you? But you can change things. Make things happen."

"Like what?" said Monique sullenly.

"My Dear! Your Nationality. Bless you!"

"Can I? How?" sulked Monique.

"Make provisions."

Monique would do anything to forsake and relinquish her German citizenship!

"My Relations will sell up and move to Spain to retire. I think I will join them," said Monique assuredly.

The Aunt clasped her hands together."

"That's it! Be positive."

Monique dreamt of Spain. The paradisiacal Balearics. Her dream of Spain kept her rather optimistic. She also fantasised about the PENINSULA. She did wish her dream would come true! (She wished to emigrate to Spain. It was such wishful thinking!) Her Spanish fantasies of Spain were exciting as well as paradisiacal.

While her Aunt went upstairs, Monique stayed downstairs in the Lounge. She rested in the armchair. She dreamt of Spain. A Spanish paradise in the Islands.

Her Aunt invited Monique to spend the night at her house. So, Monique ended up staying the night. Monique took it for granted. Unappreciating her Aunt's invitation.

Asleep that night Monique had a sweet dream!

5
The Followers of Nazism

On a cold, rainy day Monique stayed indoors. She sat on a window seat. Her elder sister Imogen stood next to her with her arms folded. Monique thought of her Nationality. She shunned being a German citizen. (Her Ancestors were Nazis and from Hitler's Youth.)

With a twitch, Monique ran her fingers through her hair. She cooled off by running her fingers through her hair. She twirled a tress around her finger. Her flaxen strands were golden. Her beautiful hair was soft, silky and shiny. Her long hair cascaded all the way down her back.

Standing in front of her sister, Imogen made a gesture.

"You are not still thinking about Nazis, are you?" gestured Sister.

Monique remained obsessed with it. It remained an obsessive preoccupation of hers.

"I get these damn rumours," mentioned Monique.

"What rumours?" asked Sister.

"I can't stand it. That I am a Nazi," replied Monique.

"Your Ancestors were once Nazis. Linz and Ladd belonged to Hitler's Youth."

"Did they really? Too damn right," said Monique sardonically.

"What are you going to do?"

"I don't know. I want to be free. I want to be free from all of this. It's just not on. I am not a Nazi. I want to live in freedom and peace," stammered Monique.

Imogen was a bigot.

"You can. Can't you."

Monique was badly distressed. In such a distressed state.

"I am not part of this. I don't swear allegiance to Hitler as my Ancestors did. I am free to choose my fate. I want my freedom. I shall get it. I am not proud. I am outraged. I am ashamed of my race," admitted Monique.

"How about a change of Nationality?" suggested Sister.

"Easier said than done. I like the idea," frowned Monique.

Meanwhile, their light-hearted Brother overheard them converse together. Tomas came in and came up to both of his pretty sisters.

"You're still not on about Nazis. Are you?" said Brother.

Staying seated Monique stayed silent.

"It's depressing. Enough of this! Let's talk about something else," suggested Imogen.

Their serious conversation about NAZISM of a controversial nature changed into another topic.

From Monique's introspection and introversion Monique became spiritual, political and radical too. Sharing her political beliefs with her family. (Including extended (Bavarian) families too.)

At once Monique left her Brother and Sister. Going upstairs to go to her bedroom alone. Monique stayed in her bedroom. She relaxed and rested. She reflected on her Ancestors. Particularly in the NAZI era at how they had been involved in NAZISM and the NAZI PARTY and at how other ones engaged in Hitler's Youth!

6
The Beer Cellar

Monique and the daughters of Brewers and Barmaids gathered together at the bottom of the beer cellar. At present there they stayed together while avoiding everybody else. At that time, they weren't intruded on nor imposed on by anybody else. In the cellar with many barrels of beer stored there everywhere, it remained claustrophobic. They could not move around due to claustrophobia. They stood still all together in a confined space. There they indulged in a pint of beer. They liked their nice treat. (It was rather similar to it being on the house.)

All of the Germans and Bavarians remained proud of themselves. Actually, quite proud of their nation, countrymen, inhabitants and being Germanic.

One Barmaid was buxom and a voluptuous Daughter of a Brewer bosomy. Her cleavage was exposed by her frilly lace white blouse unbuttoned at the top part of her blouse. Monique was a beautifully dressed up countrywoman. All of the relaxed countrywomen liked their time together. They all had the most enjoyable moments together. The thrill of it was a German speciality. A German brew. The hops had a fresh taste. All of the females were standing together in a group. It was a female affair. They did not miss having any relationships with the opposite sex or socialising together with folks and villagers. With the group gathered together. They all enjoyed their fabulous time. Their camaraderie and togetherness were like that of really good friends, and companions. With such delightful smiles, charm and personality. All of them ended up getting more joy, pleasure and bliss at being together again rather than doing anything else that night.

Later that night a Barmaid accompanied Monique back home to the German village where she lived. The buxom Barmaid was streetwise and belligerent.

7
Monique's Ambivalence

On a hot, sunny afternoon in a master bedroom. Monique stood by a wardrobe's mirrored door. She looked at herself. Catching sight of the mirrored reflection. Did she really love herself? Or hate herself? With resentment and disregard for being German. She disliked her Nationality! (Monique was aware of the xenophobia which countries have for Germany. Also, all of the xenophobic resentment for that country too!)

Having utter disrespect for it. Monique looked at her mirror image. Knowing full well she was an Arian! Without doubt. (Her Ancestors belonged to Hitler's Youth!)

Monique wasn't proud of herself. She appeared to be outraged and disgusted at being a German (citizen).

She took pride in being a Blonde beautiful female. She certainly did object to being German. She was outraged at it without question of a doubt. Particularly her Nationality! It remained a stigma and taboo being of GERMAN NATIONALITY!

She thought the history NAZISM outrageous. The Germans, NAZIS in war. Their atrocities (including extermination, executions, genocide, experimentation and war crimes).

Monique stood away from the wardrobe. Monique was startled as her Aunt suddenly appeared behind her.

The Aunt touched Monique on her shoulder with a gentle touch which was affectionate.

"My Dear! What is wrong? You can tell me."

"Everything is wrong. Me! Nothing is right. I am an Arian! I dislike being German. It's vile! I can't stand it. I loathe it you know. I don't want any part of it. I want to be free! From all this. I want to emigrate. I want to be part of another Nationality. I wish to live abroad. Will it ever happen? I wish. I don't know. What on earth am I going to do? I do depend on my relatives. I am dependent. Maybe things will change? Only time will tell," glowered Monique.

The Aunt comforted Monique with a hug. They both stood back.

"It sounds like you are distressed. By the sound of it," observed Aunt.

"Oh! I am distressed," admitted Monique.

"What have you read up on?" enquired Aunt.

"Oh! That! I am learning History. I have read up on Communism, Marxism, Fascism and Nazism. This makes me outraged. This is outrageous. I don't want any part of it. I am ashamed. Unlike my Ancestors who belonged to the Nazi Party and Hitler's Youth," said Monique ashamedly.

"Listen to me! How many times have I told you? You're not a Nazi. Don't believe it. You mustn't! You are a good citizen," reassured Aunt.

Monique suffered from trauma at being labelled as a NAZI. (Her Ancestors were members of the NAZI Party and including Hitler's Youth.)

Monique exposed and vulnerable had enough of talking to her Aunt. Monique confided in her Aunt. This time she was exasperated!

Leaving her Aunt, Monique went upstairs alone to her bedroom. She sat in an armchair. She deeply reflected on her Ancestors and her life in society in modern Germany. She was outraged at being German! Everything concerned with it quite rightly outraged her. As history is outrageous and shocking indeed. In particular NAZISM. The NAZI HISTORY itself!

Monique calmed down being alone by herself. She sat gracefully and with poise. Looking out of a window dreamily at an angle directionally opposite. She cooled down. In her shady, shadowy and cool bedroom.

8
Family Love

Today, Sunday was a hot day. Monique spent time with her Brother and Sister. Together in the Lounge they sat down and talked. Monique preferred the company of her Brother and Sister rather than her Mother. She preferred them because they remained deeply sympathetic. The sympathisers cared for their Sister!

"Aren't you going out?" asked Sister.

"No, Imogen. I'll stay in. How about you?" replied Monique.

"I am not doing anything today. I'll stay with you," smiled Sister.

Tomas popped a sweet in his mouth.

"Me. I am staying in. I am not seeing anyone," chewed Brother.

"Now have you thought things through?" asked Imogen.

"Oh! Yes. I have thought about it. Now that I have had time to reflect on it. I can now be sensible and make my decisions," answered Monique.

"What do you intend to do?" asked Sister.

Monique thought of her intentions.

"Firstly, I'd like to give up my citizenship and get a new identity and a new Nationality. Secondly, I would like to live in another country. To be free from all these stigmas," stated Monique.

Imogen wished her Sister well.

"I do hope you do it. I wish you the best of luck with it."

Monique appreciated the well-wisher. Her Sister's concern.

"I'll give it a go. I do hope so," grinned Monique.

"What's happening? asked Brother.

"Hans is keen to live abroad with his wife and daughter. He wants me to live with them," answered Monique.

"Oh! How nice. I wish you well," exclaimed Sister sweetly.

Appreciating her Sister's niceness and well-wishing. Monique kissed her Sister on her cheek.

"Thanks. I know you do," said Monique appreciatively.

Tomas patted his Sister lightly on her shoulder with affection.

"I hope it goes well for you. Will it work out?" said Brother concernedly.

Monique appreciated her Brother as a well-wisher. Wishing her well. She was deeply appreciative of his love and deep concern for her.

"I can only try. Anything is better than this. This life I am living. This stigma I dread. My life has to change. It has got to change for my sake," groaned Monique.

With concern Tomas paid heed to his Sister.

"I can only wish you well. All the best!" said Brother.

Monique, Imogen and Tomas moved to the table there where they each took a pint of beer from a tray. (Their parents were professional Brewers. They provided their children with a treat!)

Standing together they made a toast. The froth spilt over. They all drank the fine-quality beer. A German-made beer.

9
Cry Baby

Monique came out of her bedroom. Going downstairs she met her Brother along the stairs. From there they both went and entered the Lounge. Simultaneously, Monique and Tomas sat down in armchairs which were directly positioned opposite.

Both brother and sister sat facing each other. They both sweltered from the shining sun penetrating through the tinted sky roofs and big windows. The lounge was a radiant blaze. They both sweltered in the heat.

"What are your views on Nazis?" asked Brother.

Monique thought of the question.

"That's a good question. Well. What do I think? Our Ancestors were once from Hitler's Youth! Weren't they? At the rally, the German people were patriotic and fanatical. From the populace such fanaticism and patriotism. It so happened that Nazi Germany, Third Reich was a tyranny. How can you explain this? The terror by the S.S. All of the murders, disappearances, executions and takeover by the Führer. Frankly, I am ashamed of being German and of its history. I would like to be free from all of this. Who wouldn't? I would like to be another Nationality. I would do anything to emigrate to get out of here. This country. To live in Spain. A peninsula. In paradise!" blurted out Monique.

Tomas listened to his defiant sister. Respecting his sister's endeavour and aspiration.

"You are still young. You will have time to fulfil it. Haven't you considered emigration?"

"I have given it thought. It's something I have got to work on in the future. No more Nazi for me. It's something I have got to work for."

"Seeing is believing. Too much talk. Not enough action," said Brother sardonically.

"I do agree with what you say. I must put it into action," said Sister assuredly.

Monique was overcome with emotion. Monique was feeling pent-up with anger and outrage. Monique got up from the armchair. She hurried out of the lounge. Straightaway she went back upstairs to her bedroom where she locked herself in. A protective measure. She threw herself down on her bed. Falling on her bed. She began to cry. Crying like a child – and a little girl as well.

"I hate you! I hate all of you!" blubbered Monique.

10

Both Sisters Run Over to Church

Arriving home, Monique expected her sister to be waiting for her. Monique was punctual at arriving back. Monique came into the Lounge. Monique sat down in the armchair. Facing her sister who also sat down after waiting for her to come in. Imogen was seated in the armchair positioned opposite. In the shade, Monique sat cooling down in the shady coolness. From a half-open window, the breezy fresh air permeated the air-freshened lounge. She felt invigorated by the cool fresh air. She breathed in the air. She was delighted by the delightful freshness of the cool air. The weather became oppressive as hours passed by. The air was sultry and the scorching heat unbearable and sticky as time passed by.

"You're not going to go on about being a Nazi. Are you?" simpered sister.

"No. I am not. It's offensive being called a Nazi and it's fearful too," said Monique calmly.

"Our Ancestors were Nazis. Weren't they? That is debatable. Isn't it?" questioned sister.

Monique thought of the Nazi regime.

"Must we go on and live in terror and fear?" said Monique anxiously.

"No. We shouldn't. That's why we must make changes to our lives," insisted sister.

Fearing for their safety and having anxieties. Both sisters left their house to go down the road where there the local church was located near a corner of a dirty road. At that time, they both found the entrance of the church locked.

They decided to stay together out in the churchyard. For some time they lounged about. They calmed down, cooled down and pacified. Both sisters were peaceful, peaceable and protected out in the churchyard. Walking along the ground. Admiring the lovely church grounds. Passing by the gravestones everywhere there. They paid heed to the headstones and their epitaphs. They both read the inscriptions on the stone and marble gravestones.

Leaving the church. The local parish both together. They both felt rather protected, defended and protected as well as regenerated and spiritual too. They both headed back down the road. Sisters walking alongside each other on the pavement when making their short way back home.

"Yes! It's no more Nazi for us," declared Monique triumphantly.

"Hurrah!" they exclaimed victoriously.

Both of them developed faith in their Lord which protected them. Their fear of evil was allayed and anger subsided.

Monique remained optimistic about her future. Her general outlook and optimism. She gained determination from her motivation. Her motivational intentions!

Her aspirations were positive indeed. The decisions she made were well thought out.

11

Family Holiday
(A Blissful Paradise)

Monique boarded the Airliner with her family. At once all of the passengers took their seats for this European short-haul flight. This Airliner departed from GERMANY to MALAGA.

After the short flight, the Airliner landed at MALAGA Airport as scheduled. All of the passengers got off the Airliner. The crowds and crowds of passengers were transported to the busy Airport. A Terminal.

At Passport Control and CUSTOMS, all the passengers showed their passports, then they waited for a time to get their luggage from a conveyor belt. Leaving the crowded Airport, the passengers travelled to get to their destinations. The excited Holidaymakers looked forward to their holiday.

Meanwhile, Monique, her Mother, Brother and Sister impatiently waited inside the Airport near the entrance. Suddenly, the professional Driver came and picked up the family. The stout Driver took them to the minibus which was parked outside the Airport. The Driver put all their stacked luggage inside the minibus. The Driver set off on his journey. The Driver drove the passengers to the hotel.

Reaching their hotel, they entered with their luggage. The family came up to Reception. The Receptionist attended to them. They checked in at the hotel. The Receptionist led them to a lift on the Ground Floor. The porter brought up their luggage.

In the lift, they went up to their floor. They all got out of the lift and walked down the long corridor. The Receptionist showed them to their hotel rooms.

Monique took the time to admire her beautiful hotel room. The others followed suit. By admiring their hotel rooms and the views from the balcony.

Suffering from jet lag Monique rested on her bed. She took a nap. She felt better from resting. She got up and drew the curtains. The sun shone on her face. She opened the patio door and walked out onto the balcony. There she overlooked the swimming pool. She saw sunbathers sunbathing by the poolside and a few who paraded. There were a few women in the swimming pool. One of them swam.

Monique still felt too enervated. She lacked the energy and enthusiasm to do anything. She sat on a chair and took the time to rest. Her inclination for love was romantic. Her tendency for romance was an obsessive wishful notion. How she obsessed with love!

Her obsession with love was a wishful desire and whim. Monique felt too uncomfortable. She got up and lay down on her bed again. Feeling comfortable from lying down in comfort. She took a siesta. She still suffered from fatigue and jet lag.

Monique must have dreamt. She had a beautiful dream.

Suddenly Monique, half-asleep and half-awake, heard loud knocks on her hotel door. She got up from her bed. She walked barefoot towards the door. Monique opened the door.

"Are you coming? We are going out for a walk," said sister impatiently.

Now Monique expected her sister to come. She remained unprepared to go out.

"Hang on. Not now. Now is not the time. I had such a lovely dream. It's wonderful. So unbelievable. I can't explain it. I can't describe it. I love it here. I love this country. I have to get out of my country. It is degrading. You are dehumanised. It's a stigma. It's too controversial for me. I can't stand the controversy. The sooner I leave this country the better. I can't live where I am living. I have to get out. I must be free. This country is beautiful. I envy it. There is such freedom and peace here. It is a paradise. I have been given a lifeline. My Relative is moving to Spain. Hans wants me to move in and live with his Wife and Daughter. I am no longer living a fantasy. It is a reality. I am not living in a dream world of mine. The dream is real," said Monique honestly.

"Are you coming?" prompted sister.

"No. You go. I will stay here."

Monique closed the door as Imogen her sister left. Monique feeling tired had to lie down on her bed. She felt lazy and idle as she lounged about. Monique ended up staying in her hotel room for hours. She was far too tired to do anything else today. She thought of Spain in her dreams. She fantasised about the wonders and delights of MENORCA (MINORCA). The paradise of Spain. The paradisiacal beauty of Spain and its beautiful islands. She dreamt of the Peninsula.

Monique spent her time dreaming of Spain. It's the marvellous beauty of paradise. The Balearic Islands. How wonderful it is!

Monique was sitting in the armchair in a position of comfort. Monique feeling sleepy had dozed off. Later Monique awoke. She showered and got dressed to go out to the restaurant with her family. When she was ready. She sat on a chair while patiently waiting for her sister to call on her at her hotel door. With expected anticipation meeting together on the ground floor. Altogether the family went to the restaurant where the diners dined at the reserved table.

At the table, Monique felt nauseous. She hardly talked. She also only ate about half her dinner due to being queasy. At that time Monique stayed in the restaurant for only about half an hour before leaving to go back to her hotel room.

Monique spent time lying down on her bed resting. Monique was deeply thinking of Spain. It's a fine paradise. It's a way of life. Its culture, history, etiquette, custom and traditions. She desired such wonders!

On the first night of her holiday. Staying at the hotel. Monique went to bed early. Keeping away from her family. Wanting to be alone to recover from jet lag.

Sometime early in the morning, Monique had breakfast in bed. Her Mother treated her Daughter to it. Monique was delighted at the nice surprise of it. Expecting it, Monique had room service that morning. She enjoyed her nice treat. After having eaten her breakfast in bed and drunk her cup of tea. She had a lie-in.

During the day Monique insisted to her Mother that she intended to relax as usual throughout today. She wasn't keen on doing any exercise. She remained undisciplined. She did not want to exert herself.

A few hours later in the daytime, Monique indulged in the Jacuzzi. A thrilling pleasure. She took a thrill from her pleasure of eroticism. She engaged in erotomania as the Female sex does. She took pleasure from her self-indulgence. Her over-indulgence was extremely excessive. She had a thrill as she engaged in eroticism. Her sensualism was Feminine!

The water felt soothing to her skin, it was a pleasurable sensation, a delightful pleasure. Monique relaxed in the Jacuzzi. Enjoying her relaxation and pleasure. It was such a delightful joy. One in which she had been self-indulgent and abandoned herself. She was lost in her fantasies. Her ecstasies of thrill! She experienced peace, joy and freedom. Where else could she find this? Her abandonment was a pleasure. Her pain was assuaged and her tension soothed. She relaxed for a long time. Enjoying her pleasure of relaxation. Her leisure a preoccupation.

As soon as the professional manicurist had done Imogen's manicure, Imogen joined her sister in the sauna. Spaced out both sisters sat in a sauna with a thick bath towel tightly wrapped around their bodies. The sauna steamed up. The condensation rose. They both perspired in the heat. This was the first time they both had a sauna together. They both experienced something new. It was a new experience. They both took satisfying pleasure from their sauna. It was satisfyingly pleasurable. They both steamed up in the hot sauna. The heat was too hot. They both sweated and dehydrated. They both felt rather thirsty. Perspiring in the heat. Feeling the heat they could not see each other in the thick steam rising in the air, despite sitting close to one another. Monique was sweating. Her untanned body looked beautiful. Her younger sister Imogen was rather too shy to expose herself in the nude. Imogen felt inhibited. Imogen's childish inhibition was quite evident to her sister who unnoticed it and her exhibitionism.

Monique got more joy at being alone with her sister than doing anything else. She enjoyed spending time with her sister. It was a thrilling joy. As it was something new they experienced. Both sisters felt faint in the heat. They both tried to get used to it.

"I like it here. There is such peace and freedom here. You don't get it anywhere else," said Monique softly.

"It's nice. I love it. I can't get enough of it. This is the life. Why can't we have a life like this? The jet set and elite do. Don't they?" said sister enviously.

Monique sighed in relief.

"It's good to be free. Some day when I am free I shan't look back."

Leaving the spa and sauna both sisters left each other when reaching the floor where their hotel rooms were.

Monique wearily went back to her hotel room. She drank plenty of mineral water from out of a plastic bottle. She felt too tired and enervated. There she rested in bed for about an hour. She recovered during her time of resting.

Monique spent most of her day in her hotel room relaxing. With no motive or intention to do anything else for the rest of the day.

On Tuesday afternoon, Monique and her family went to the beach. It was within walking distance. This particularly sandy beach was beautiful in this sunny region.

Today the beach was crowded with people. There were holidaymakers, couples, families and children.

They walked down the beach, finding it crowded everywhere. They all stopped as they came to somewhere isolated and secluded. They all stopped at this secluded spot and sat down on the sand. They admired the view of the lovely beach from sitting and standing. They relaxed together. With discomfort and unease, they lounged about. Admiring the beauty of this beach. They breathed in the sultry sea breeze. They sweltered from the blazing sun shining. They felt discomfort at sitting in an uncomfortable position for a long time. They all got up and stood still. They stretched out. They all walked down the rocky parts of the beach. The sea washed up on the shore. Walking along near the shore they came across barefooted female Spaniards wearing swimsuits emerging out from behind the rocks and a stream of water running from there. As they reached as far as they could towards a dead end. They all turned back and headed back all the way to their hotel. They did not stay too long at the beach today as it was far too crowded with holidaymakers.

Going to the ground floor where the Reception was, Mother and Daughter sat down in the seating area. They both flicked through magazines while Monique and her Brother took the lift to their hotel rooms.

Monique lay down on her bed and rested. Hours later she entered a spa. She indulged in a luxury spa. She relaxed in a spa. Her body felt soothed from the bubbles of water. She took pleasure from the self-indulgence of relaxing in a spa, a luxury and pleasurable thrill. Her enjoyment of pleasure was a sheer delight. Feeling light-headed she abandoned herself in a spa. She took thrilling delight as she enjoyed herself in the spa. She enjoyed the pleasure of luxury. In the pool, the marble spa had jets of water pumping. She felt thrilled at having such sensual pleasure. She enjoyed her abandonment, freedom and peace. It made a difference to her circumstances. Her pleasurable sensualism.

Getting out of a spa. With a bath towel, she thoroughly dried herself until her body dried. Then she got dressed. Her flaxen hair was wet. Her make-up was really beautiful indeed. Her blusher, rouge translucent.

Monique went back to her hotel room. She dried her hair naturally using a towel. From a natural way of drying not using a blow dryer.

Sitting on an easy chair, Monique rested in her hotel room. Enjoying her time alone again. She got some peace and quiet. Though she did hear doors slamming, opening and closing somewhere along the corridor.

Monique already dressed and prepared had waited for her sister to come and get her. At 7 pm, Monique dined with her family at the hotel restaurant. Then straight afterwards she stayed in her hotel room and watched television in bed. Monique took comfort as she lounged. Then went to bed at 10 pm. That night she had a peaceful sleep. It was by far her best night's sleep. She dreamt a sweet dream!

On Wednesday, Monique and her Mother and Sister spent most of the day on the beach, except for Tomas who only spent about an hour at the beach before going back to the hotel.

Monique sunbathed to get a lovely suntan. Her dark tan was bronze. Monique enjoyed her time as she lounged about on the beach. She pleased herself by sunbathing. The sunbather gratified herself as she engaged in eroticism. With libido and desire, she indulged in female sensualism.

After sunbathing for hours. Monique attracted desire and attention as she paraded like an elegant model! She remained nonchalant and narcissistic. For Monique sunbathing on the Spanish beach, today remained a highlight for her. She desired to get in the limelight! Her experience was a good one. Monique felt deeply emotional when the children came onto the beach together to play. They all made a sandcastle within reach ashore. Monique was impressed at the sandcastle the children made. The sight of it was impressive. The big sandcastle had finely-made battlements and a moat filled up with water. Monique never got the chance to play with the children. She felt deep regret and disappointment towards them.

Monique was tempted to join in and help them to make a sandcastle. Due to being a Foreigner and too shy. She was unable to participate in helping them make a sandcastle. She shook with nerves finding them all alone together with buckets and spades.

She felt saddened when the group of sweet children had gone. She waved goodbye to all of them just before they all left in a hurry. With giggles and smiles all of the happy children acknowledged the emotional holidaymaker's wave to them. With deep respect, they remembered her. They also had high regard for the Foreigner.

On that hot day, a Spanish raving beauty eclipsed her. The senorita attracted attention. This graceful and elegant Spaniard passing by had been desired and adored. She was the loveliest, most desirable, sexiest and most appealing countrywoman there on this beach today.

Getting back to the Hotel, Monique rested in her bed. Very late in the afternoon, she met her sister in her hotel room. She had some latitude at being with Imogen for a short time. Monique had been latitudinal in her principles and outlook. Alone in her hotel room. She stayed in there all alone. She had been deeply contemplative and reflective.

She kept herself occupied by reading a summer romance. She then got tired of reading the novel. She put it down on the floor. Monique rested on the easy chair. When it was time to go, Imogen came to get her sister. They joined the rest of their family waiting for them at the restaurant.

Eating her dinner Monique worried about her diet. She ate too much starch and carbohydrates in her diet. She suffered from vitamin deficiency and also her cholesterol was too high.

She realised she had to diet and slim as well as discipline herself to engage in exercise.

Afterwards, Monique had been the only one excused to leave the table first. Her Mother agitated her

Daughter about discipline. The necessary importance of it, to take disciplinary measures.

Monique eluded and avoided her family. She stayed the rest of her time in her hotel room watching television in bed.

The next day the Tourists went sightseeing.

The following day after that they took a hike down the trails and beaten tracks by following its route.

On the last few days, they took a tour, a ride on a bus around the region of the city. Then followed by shopping around in boutiques and a supermarket and then stopped off at a café. They finally rounded it off almost on the last day of their holiday by dining out at a restaurant in a square.

12
A Miracle (Dream)

One night Monique felt deeply unhappy, miserable and depressed. Her Mother a depressive!

She thought it was wise to pray. She took the opportunity to pray. She knelt down and prayed. She pleaded to the Lord thy God for mercy.

"Lord help me. I am a mess. My life is a mess. What life do I have as a German? I am unemployed. I am a Blonde model material. I have no future. I am too exposed, vulnerable and miserable. As a last resort, I make my plea to you. I plead to you Father God for mercy. I pray for you to transform my life. Please make a transformation in my life. Make me spiritual and blessed. Provide for me. Love me! And look after me. Take care of me. I surrender my soul to you. I offer myself to you. I sacrifice myself to you. I have no life here in this country. I pray Hans will take me in at his new place and his Wife and Daughter accept me. Love me! Please Lord make my dreams come true. Literally, I have nothing. I have only got you now. Please help me. Make me happy. Give me happiness and joy. I ask for this. Make my life productive and stable. Give me stability and love too. Make my life deeply meaningful, profound and productive. Protect me from evil. Have mercy on me and my life of course. Give me a miracle.

Lord I really do need it right now. Thank you, heavenly Father. Amen."

Monique got up from her stiff knees. She stood up and stretched out. She ached with a spasm. Her pain was assuaged. She felt comforted by praying. Her fears were allayed.

    Wearing her black nightdress, Monique got into bed. Stretching out she switched off a lamp on top of the chest of drawers in the far corner.

    That night Monique slept well. Sound asleep. She had a beatific paradise dream. With a miracle!

13
Monique's Introspective

In the study, Monique sat on a swivel chair at the desk. She spent time looking at a reference book. Suddenly Tomas entered the study. Monique was disturbed by her Brother entering. She lost her concentration on reading. Something else distracted Monique.

"Tell me. It's not the Nazis you are reading up on?"

"It is. In fact, it's the Nazis I am reading up on," answered Monique.

"Oh! No! Not the Nazis," paused Brother. "What have you learned?"

Monique learned about Second World War History.

"Hitler conquered Europe. Didn't he? He invaded Europe. The countries were under Nazi occupation," paused Monique.

"And. What else?" prompted Brother.

"There were atrocities, war crimes, mass murders, genocide, experimentations. The SS. Gestapo. What else?" paused Monique. "Regarding being German, I am ashamed of it. It is an outrage and disgrace. History repeats itself. I dislike being German. I want to be free. I want to be another race or nationality. Anything is better than this torment, and stigma. It would be far better to live abroad and change my Nationality. Quite frankly I have had enough of it. Enough is enough. I can't stand it. Living abroad will be the best thing for me. My best option. I do hope you understand with regards to how I feel about it," grimaced Monique.

"You can only try," said Brother.

"Try I will."

Monique closed a reference book. She got up and hurried out of the study. Leaving her Brother to muse on. Monique remained irritable and annoyed at the intrusion of her Brother into the study. Monique went upstairs. She stayed in her bedroom. In comfort, she sat down in the armchair facing the window opposite. There the broad daylight was bright.

She reflected on her Ancestors. She felt shame at how her Ancestors were once Nazis and also from Hitler's Youth.

Monique would give up her Nationality with deliberate intention. She intended to do so with discretion. Monique would be making plans so much better than doing anything else. She gained solace from an up-to-date update from Hans her Relative. Monique was instantly reassured. From Hans' confirmation of progression. Hans made progress. Her life appeared to be so much better. Now her future remained bright. Monique was feeling rather happy and optimistic.

14
Monique's Nazi Recrimination

At a friend's house, Monique stayed together with a group of her friends. Monique stayed quiet. At that present time, Monique preferred not to join in the conversation nor converse with any of them. Her nice and unpleasant friends remained chatty as usual. Monique preferred to isolate herself from her sociable friends talking. Monique got up and sat in an armchair away from them, positioned on the other side of the Lounge.

One of her friends, a trainee, called out to her. Miss Smid threw a purse.

"Here you are. Get it! You are not still doing the Nazi thing. Are you?"

In a state of disquiet, Monique felt disturbed and disrupted. Monique picked up her purse.

"Me! No! I am reading up on it. I am learning about it. I have got some knowledge from it," replied Monique.

Miss Smid tutted. "Your Ancestors, Nazis!" said Miss Smid provocatively.

With disdain and defiance, Monique protested. Arguing her case against it.

"I do believe they were. They were from Hitler's Youth too. Personally, I don't believe in it. I am outraged and ashamed of it. I just can't go on living with Nazi recriminations. I must get out of here. This country! I was thinking of changing my Nationality and living abroad."

"That's a hard thing to do. Stay focused. Well best of luck," wished Miss Smid.

"Wish me well," shrugged Monique.

Miss Smid acknowledged her experiences with it. The common stigmas of being German and the taboo of the aftermath of Germany losing the First and Second World Wars.

"We all go through the same thing. Don't we? We all live through it. It's our History. We should be proud of our culture and heritage. It has always been like this. Germany strives to be a great Nation."

Monique raised an objection to it.

"The History, it's downright heinous. It's debased. Damn it! Damn History!" objected Monique.

"We can't change History. How can we? We still can aim to be a great Nation!" believed Miss Smid.

Monique thought Miss Smid was self-opinionated.

"I do agree with what you say. Yet how can we? Germany is a defeated Nation. Isn't it? This Nation can strive for greatness. Me. I won't be around to live it, to tell the tale. I am getting out of here. I am living somewhere else. Anything is better than here."

"Surely it can't be too bad," groaned Steff.

"Oh! It is. It's diabolical. It's accursed. A curse."

"Germany does well," remarked Steff.

"Does it. That's debatable. I guess it does well in some things," commented Monique.

"Don't put Germany down. Be proud! Let's strive to be great," remonstrated Miss Smid.

"For Germany, it is a debasement. It is vile. For Germany as a Nation," said Monique ashamedly.

"This Nation can be great. There is hope. Isn't there," said Steff unashamedly.

Monique's friends remained patriotic and rather too proud of their Nation while Monique seemed to be outraged by it. She raised objections again. It's objectionable. Finding it provocative. With Monique showing contempt, indignation and grievance. The Nation's History is a national outcry and its civilisation. Its provocation is a heinous outrageousness!

Presently Monique sat gracefully with her graceful legs crossed on the armchair. Staying there alone without the rest of her friends joining her or at present bothering to engage in any further conversation with her. Monique stayed with all her friends until it was time to go. To get back home. Coming to terms with it as normal. She got outraged at it. The outrageous and abominable Nazism in a war era of GERMAN HISTORY and civilisation.

Footnote

One day Monique read a History Textbook (this textbook had never been returned to its Department).

Hitler's War. The Red Army liberated Berlin in April 1945. The Nazis surrendered.

Several months later

Nowadays Monique had a chance to start a new life abroad. To live a Spanish lifestyle on the Peninsula!

Now, will she ever gain peace and freedom? Will her miseries and troubles ever end from now on?

15
Monique's Punctual Departure

Monique embraced her Mother and Brother and Sister. She said farewell to all of them. A parting. Her family. Monique was already prepared to leave and got in a car and her Uncle drove her to the Airport.

At the Departure Lounge Monique waited. All of the passengers departed. The passengers got on board the Airliner.

Hours later at the Airport Monique met Hans and his attractive Wife waiting for her near the entrance of the Airport.

Monique embraced Hans and his Wife passionately. Hans and his slender Wife led Monique to their car. Monique got in the car. She was driven to their home.

Hans and his Wife showed Monique around their house. Monique looked around their house. She greatly admired their lovely townhouse.

"Well. What do you think?" asked Hans.

"It's really lovely. I love it," replied Monique.

"How are you feeling?" asked Wife.

Monique exaggerated. A genuine reaction of hers.

"It's great. I never felt so much happiness in all of my life!" exclaimed Monique deliriously.

"Tell me something. You talk about Peninsula. What is that to you?" asked Relative.

"Hans, it's a beautiful land. Really it is! It's really somewhere wonderful. I often dream of it. I will get there," said Monique dreamily.

Hans smiled. A broad smile.

"You will. Will you? Let us show you," said Hans happily.

Subsequently, Monique moved in. She looked forward to starting her new life here in sunny Spain. She made new friends. She travelled.

Monique lived a truly wonderful life here. A good lifestyle. She did not look back!

Asleep one night Monique dreamt of a beach of dreams. A Spanish Paradise!

She had such a beautiful natural dream. A wonderful Paradise dream!

Naturally, her dream included both a beautiful beach and a paradisaic PENINSULA at which she had a memorable walkabout.

Did Monique dream? Or was her imagination just a wild dream!

16
Cosmopolitan Citizen (Spanish Days and Life)

Monique's life in Spain was rather different from how her life used to be in Germany. It was peaceful, civilised and cultural. The Spaniards Monique met were friendly, kind, caring and considerate. She took siestas during the daytime. Customarily she got used to it. She loved Spanish culture, tradition, etiquette, custom, fashion, and heritage. She liked Spanish food and drink, nightlife, music, arts and entertainment and tourism. She learned about Spanish History. How Spain remained neutral in the Second World War.

Living with her relative, Hans, his Wife and Daughter was a blessing and a great feeling. They accommodated and provided for Monique. Monique loved them. She loved her new life in Spain. She was free now. She desired her independence. Trying to be independent proved to be difficult as she was an exposed foreign citizen who remained vulnerable and peaceful about civilisation.

She learned about Spanish fashion. She dressed up the Spanish way. She modelled clothes in her spare time. (With an interest in modelling she had a passion for clothes.)

A stunning natural beauty with an amazing look. A natural look and poise when dressed up and photographed. The beauty was photogenic.

Monique settled down to her new life in the PENINSULA. She loved her life. She enjoyed her peace, freedom and privacy. She struggled to speak the Spanish language to communicate. She took the time to learn the Spanish language.

She discovered the mysteries of Spain. Its great wonder, delight and sheer beauty of it. The great charm of its pleasantness.

Monique became cultured, an aesthete and a natural connoisseur! She developed a great interest in the arts, food and drink, fashion, music and dance (flamenco).

Monique became happier, beatific and blissful at living near a village near the PENINSULA. Monique felt a deep beatitude!

One day Monique met Hans' friend, a Spaniard. Monique found it extremely difficult to communicate with this Spaniard. His dialect a Catalan.

She learned from her experience of meeting the stranger. Typically meeting strangers remained difficult, something new and strange. She had to learn from it. The Foreigner was embarrassed at struggling to speak (fluent) Spanish.

Monique learned about Spanish beach life. She loved to go to the lovely beaches. It was her favourite thing. It was an enjoyable interest and preoccupation of hers. She was obsessed with beaches and nightlife. It was a good obsession of hers. She took wonder and delight at the beautiful beaches. At times she lived a secluded life. Though she did make the effort to dress up beautifully and hence meet people. She took an interest in the prospect of meeting people. It was a good prospect.

Monique learned to travel too around the regions of Spain. Travelling was an interest of hers and tourism and sightseeing of course.

On one hot, sunny day at the back of a finca in a doorway, Monique stepped out of the back door. She wore a beautiful red silk and satin (Spanish) dress. The beautiful material felt silky and satiny. It tumbled down to the ground. It draped beautifully with impeccable immaculateness.

She looked glamorous!

She enjoyed the glamour. She looked stunning. The German Blonde Spaniard!

Standing in the blaze. She was blinded by the blazing light. There standing in a position she overlooked the Peninsula in the distance.

17
Monique's Beach Life and Times at Peninsula

Monique enjoyed her Spanish beach life. She ended up going to the beach. She spent short days or long days on beaches. All depended on the summer weather forecast and weather conditions. Monique liked to spend her time with the Spaniards on the beach. It gave her such great pleasure. She got more joy at being with them than anything else. (Except for the natural Peninsula of course which made her beatific, blissful and delirious!)

On the beach, Monique lounged. She was thrilled with pleasure at relaxing, sunbathing herself. Her body was suntanned. She desired to get noticed, wanting to attract attention. She desired to fulfil her modelling pursuits. Her aspiration for modelling shoots and modelling assignments became a fulfilment.

Surrounding her were most likely Spaniards. They would come to the beach as they were accustomed to it. It was something of a customary leisure of theirs. Monique lay on the sandy beach while sunbathing.

Closing her eyes, she heard the sounds of the atmospheric sensations of the sea. The waves of the sea.

Monique felt so peaceful, tranquil, restful and relaxed. She enjoyed the beauty of paradise! She marvelled at its delights. Its naturally wonderful surroundings. The sandy beach was beautiful. It was heavenly and paradisiacal. The sun shone. The dazzling golden sand was thick, pure, coarse and hot. The sun shone with golden resplendence. The beach was so hot. The temperature rising in Fahrenheit.

Feeling dry and thirsty, Monique was dehydrated and sweated. With luxury suntan lotion applied to her skin, Monique naturally tanned. She enjoyed the pleasure of sunbathing. The sunbather indulged in relaxation. She took pleasurable enjoyment from suntanning herself.

The glorious sunny weather shone hotter. It was hottest in mid-afternoon in the Mediterranean. Monique liked to sunbathe. She enjoyed her pleasure. Her solitude, freedom, abandonment and peace and quiet.

With gratified pleasure, she was satisfied at suntanning her body. Her body was dark bronze. Her tanned skin was beautiful. Her beautiful golden hair and pubes were glossy, silky and shiny.

Monique nodded off. Her time of peaceful relaxation on the beach that day lasted hours. She was unaware of everything. She was oblivious to almost everything around her. She was lost in a dream. A paradise sea and beach dream of blissful nature. A beatific sunbather who sunbathed, and enjoyed herself in delirious pleasure!

After spending most of the day sunbathing, Hans picked up Monique and drove her home. Quite a long journey. The passenger sitting in the passenger seat in wonder. Monique felt elated, overjoyed, jubilant and ecstatic. She took wonder at her dream. Her vision!

Reaching home, Monique got out of the car quickly. She ran into the townhouse. Going into her bedroom. She locked herself in her bedroom. She turned the key in a lock on the bedroom door. She threw herself down on her bed, a mattress close by. She took a rest.

18

A Peninsula Dream

On a hot day, Monique and Hans and her family took a hike to a Peninsula. There she enjoyed her time on the Peninsula. She had a fabulous time. At that present time, Monique felt much calmer, quieter, peaceable and cooler.

She cherished her precious time at the wonderful Peninsula. At once realising this place and land was a beautiful Paradise! It was a dream location setting. Truly today at this PENINSULA remained a memorable memory of hers. She never forgot her deep memory. Her remembered dream of the PENINSULA that sultry summer night.

- THE END -

Also by S.M. Flanagan

*Available worldwide from Amazon
and all good bookstores*

www.mtp.agency

www.facebook.com/mtp.agency

@mtp_agency

www.ingramcontent.com/pod-product-compliance
Lightning Source LLC
LaVergne TN
LVHW051217070526
838200LV00063B/4938